The Biggest Apple Ever

The Biggest Apple Ever

by Steven Kroll

illustrated by Jeni Bassett

Cartwheel BOOKS®

SCHOLASTIC INC.

New York Toronto London Auckland Sydney Mexico City New Delhi Hong Kong

For Kathleen – S.K.

Text copyright © 2011 by Steven Kroll.
Illustrations copyright © 2011 by Jeni Bassett.

Library of Congress Cataloging-in-Publication Data
Kroll, Steven.
The biggest apple ever / by Steven Kroll ; illustrated by Jeni
Bassett. – 1st ed.
p. cm.
Summary: Clayton and Desmond work together to try to find the biggest
apple for a school contest, but when realize they will not win they find
a better use for all of the apples they have collected.
ISBN 978-0-545-24836-5 (pbk.)
[1. Mice–Fiction. 2. Apples–Fiction. 3. Cookery–Apples–Fiction. 4.
Cooperativeness–Fiction. 5. Schools–Fiction.] I. Bassett, Jeni, ill. II. Title.

PZ7.K9225Bjms 2011
[E]–dc22

2010014616

ISBN 978-0-545-24836-5

10 9 8 7 6 5 4 3 2 1   11 12 13 14 15

Printed in the U.S.A.   40
First Edition, August 2011
Designed by Angela Jun

Once there were two mice who fell in love with the same apple pie, but you had to be there to see how it happened.

On opening day at Mouseville School, the principal, Mr. Mouser, made an announcement.

"We will be learning about apples this fall, and to get things started, we will have a contest. Whoever brings in the biggest apple to his teacher will win a special prize.

The judging will take place on Friday. Good luck to everyone."

"I have an apple tree in my backyard," said Penelope. "I bet it has really big apples."

"There's an apple tree across from my house," said James. "I'm going to climb it as soon as I get home."

"I don't have any apple trees," said Clayton, the house mouse, "but I'm going to find Mrs. Mousely the biggest apple ever."

"No, you're not," said his friend Desmond, the field mouse, "I am."

"Oh, yeah?" said Clayton.

"Yeah," said Desmond.

All the way home on the school bus, Clayton and Desmond talked about the contest.

"Maybe I could grow an apple tree with really big apples," said Clayton.

"It takes too long," said Desmond. "I heard Mrs. Mousely say six years."

"I'll think of something," said Clayton.

"So will I," said Desmond.

When Clayton got off the bus,
he sneaked back into town to see what
Penelope and James were up to.

Penelope had come down
from her tree. She was carrying two
tiny apples.

James was still up in the tree across the street. He was picking very small apples.

Clayton knew he'd seen bigger ones at the market.

When Desmond came by a little later, he realized the same thing.

The next day at school, Penelope and James brought in their tiny apples. No one else had brought in anything.

Mrs. Mousely cleared her throat. "Class, we have a lot of work to start the year, but because we are learning about apples and having an apple contest, we will go to Barnaby's Orchard this afternoon."
Everyone got very excited.

"I'm going to find the winning apple," said Clayton.
"*I'm* going to find the winning apple," said Desmond.

At the orchard, Mrs. Mousely pointed out the different kinds of apples. Then everyone disappeared into the trees, looking for a winner.

Clayton walked down one row, craning his neck.
Desmond walked down another row, craning his neck.
Then Clayton saw what he thought was a really big apple. It was a little too high to reach, but he stretched for it.

At that moment, Desmond saw the very same apple on the very same branch. He stretched for it too.

They bumped heads and fell down.

"I think we should bring this apple in together," said Clayton.

"No one said we couldn't," said Desmond.

But when they got back to the bus, James had an apple that was even bigger. The apple was so big, he could hardly carry it.

Clayton and Desmond looked at each other. What would they do now?

That night at dinner, Clayton explained the problem to his dad.

"Hmm," said Dad, "apples don't come in too many sizes. Do you think you'll find a bigger one?"

"I don't know," said Clayton.

"Then maybe James will win the prize this time. It's okay if he does."

Over at Desmond's house, Uncle Vernon said exactly the same thing.

But Clayton and Desmond were still determined.

The next afternoon, they met at Barnaby's Orchard. They picked two huge baskets of apples, but nothing they found was bigger than the apple James had picked.

"You know," Clayton said, "I think Dad was right. This time James gets to win. But we've got all these apples. Why don't we bake a big apple pie?"

Desmond laughed. "Great! Let's bake the biggest apple pie ever! And we'll make it for our class!"

Clayton nodded. "And I think I know where we'll find a pie pan that's big enough."

The following afternoon, Desmond arrived at Clayton's house with Uncle Vernon.

"Everything's packed up and ready," Clayton said. "It's all in Dad's truck."

"But where are we going?" Desmond asked.

"You'll find out in a minute," said Clayton.

Dad drove, with Clayton and Desmond beside him in the front seat. Uncle Vernon stayed in back, with the apples and other ingredients for the giant pie.

As they came around a corner, Desmond gasped. "Tony's Pizza!"

"Of course," said Clayton. "What could be better than a giant pizza pan?"

Mr. Tony greeted them at the door. "Welcome! Welcome! We are ready to begin!"

And so they got to work, making the dough for the crust, kneading it, rolling out half into a big circle, and spreading it over the deep-dish pan.

Then everyone peeled and sliced the apples, mixed together the sugar and spices, and spread the rest of the dough on top.

"Wow!" said Clayton and Desmond when they were finished. "Wow, wow, wow!"

"An hour!" said Mr. Tony. "Give me an hour!" The giant pan just fit into his huge oven.

The next day was Friday. Who would have the largest apple? James of course! And Mr. Mouser handed him the prize, a cheddar cheese apple.

Mrs. Mousely looked surprised. "Clayton? Desmond? Nothing from you?"

The two of them grinned. At that same moment, the classroom door flew open. In came Clayton's dad, Uncle Vernon, and Mr. Tony, struggling to carry the giant pie by themselves.

"How wonderful!" said Mrs. Mousely. "That's the biggest apple pie ever."

"We made it for the whole class!" said Clayton.

"All of us together!" said Desmond.

They shared a high five, and everyone in the class had a very big slice.